EVERYBODY HAS A BODY

Jon Burgerman

OXFORD
UNIVERSITY PRESS

Everybody

has a body.

Some are big.

some are small.

and some are tall.

Some are weak,

some are strong.

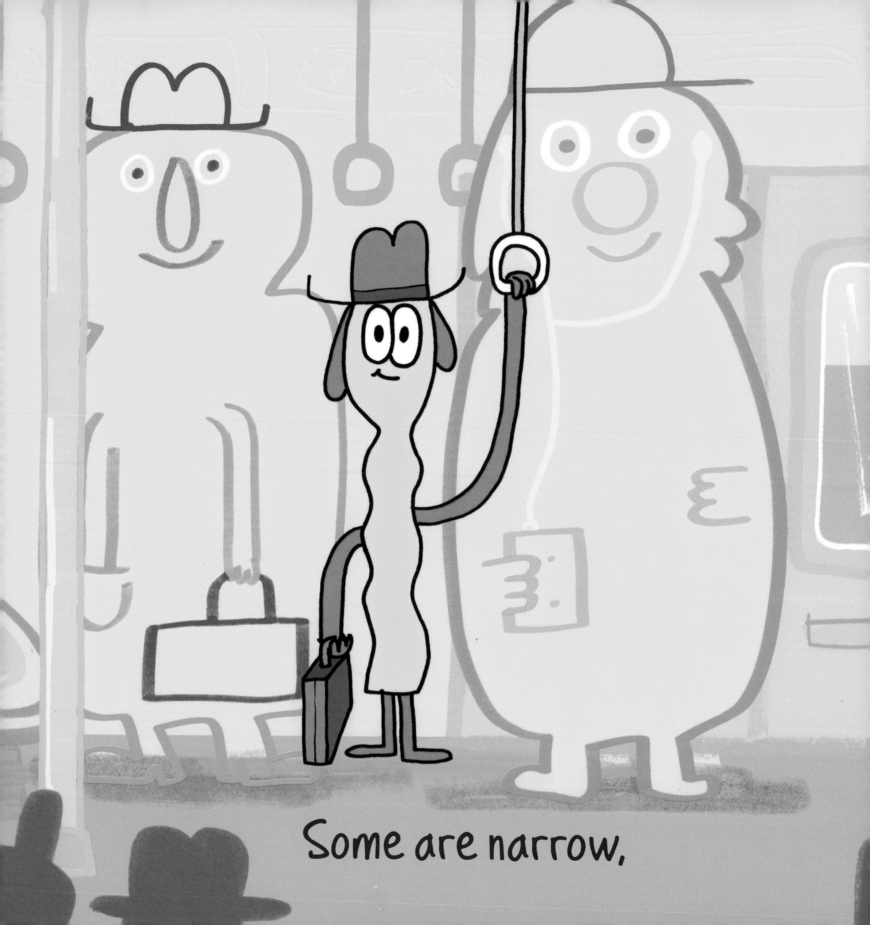

Some are narrow,

...re loooooooong.

some a

some are smooth.

Some are clumsy,

while others groove.

Some are soft,

some are rough.

Some are bendy,

and some are tough.

Some are old,

some are new.

Bodies come in

every hue.

Being different is nothing new.
It makes us special and makes you ...

You're like nobody else!

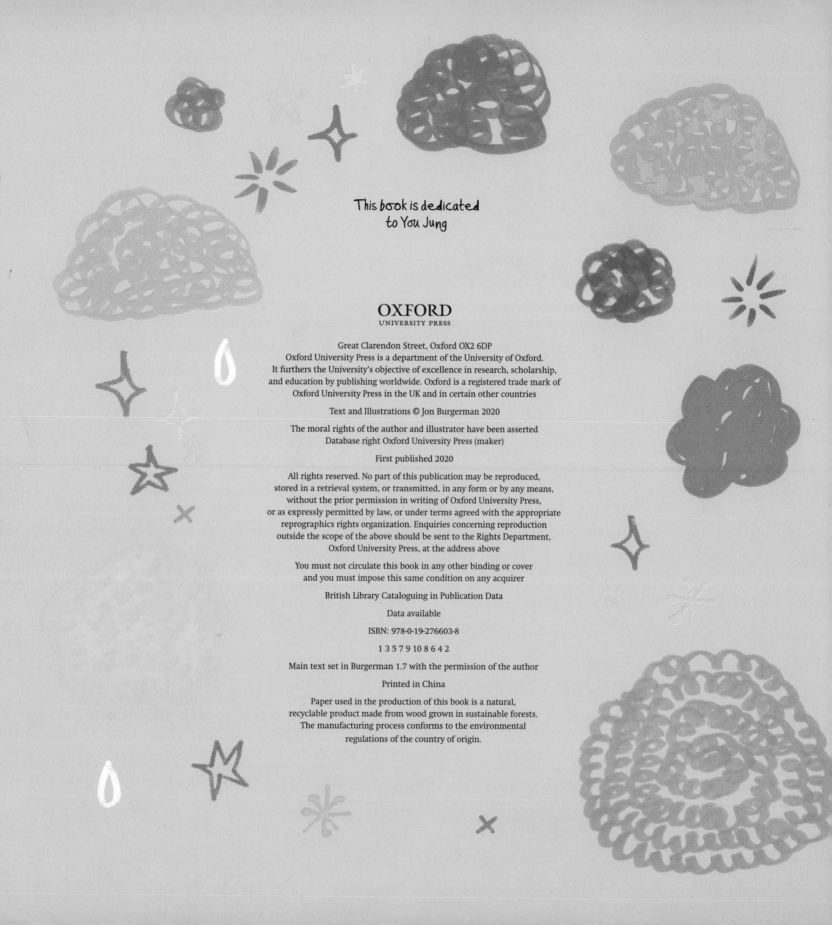

This book is dedicated
to You Jung

OXFORD
UNIVERSITY PRESS

Great Clarendon Street, Oxford OX2 6DP
Oxford University Press is a department of the University of Oxford.
It furthers the University's objective of excellence in research, scholarship,
and education by publishing worldwide. Oxford is a registered trade mark of
Oxford University Press in the UK and in certain other countries

Text and Illustrations © Jon Burgerman 2020

The moral rights of the author and illustrator have been asserted
Database right Oxford University Press (maker)

First published 2020

British Library Cataloguing in Publication Data

Data available

ISBN: 978-0-19-276603-8

1 3 5 7 9 10 8 6 4 2

Main text set in Burgerman 1.7 with the permission of the author

Printed in China

Paper used in the production of this book is a natural,
recyclable product made from wood grown in sustainable forests.
The manufacturing process conforms to the environmental
regulations of the country of origin.